2-21

P9-DMR-164

Dear Parent:
Your child's love of reading starts here!

Every child learns to read in a different way and at his or her own speed. Some go back and forth between reading levels and read favorite books again and again. Others read through each level in order. You can help your young reader improve and become more confident by encouraging his or her own interests and abilities. From books your child reads with you to the first books he or she reads alone, there are I Can Read Books for every stage of reading:

SHARED READING
Basic language, word repetition, and whimsical illustrations, ideal for sharing with your emergent reader

BEGINNING READING
Short sentences, familiar words, and simple concepts for children eager to read on their own

READING WITH HELP
Engaging stories, longer sentences, and language play for developing readers

READING ALONE
Complex plots, challenging vocabulary, and high-interest topics for the independent reader

ADVANCED READING
Short paragraphs, chapters, and exciting themes for the perfect bridge to chapter books

I Can Read Books have introduced children to the joy of reading since 1957. Featuring award-winning authors and illustrators and a fabulous cast of beloved characters, I Can Read Books set the standard for beginning readers.

A lifetime of discovery begins with the magical words **"I Can Read!"**

Visit www.icanread.com for information
on enriching your child's reading experience.

To all teachers—
especially the art teacher in college
who told me I had some talent. . . .
Your words gave me courage all these years.
—James Dean

I Can Read Book® is a trademark of HarperCollins Publishers.

Copyright © by James Dean (for the character of Pete the Cat)
Pete the Cat: Pete at the Beach
Copyright © 2013 by James Dean. All rights reserved. Manufactured in China. No part of this book may be used or reproduced in any manner whatsoever without written permission except in the case of brief quotations embodied in critical articles and reviews. For information address HarperCollins Children's Books, a division of HarperCollins Publishers, 195 Broadway, New York, NY 10007.
www.icanread.com
Library of Congress catalog card number: 2012952453
ISBN 978-0-06- 211073-2 (trade bdg.)—ISBN 978-0-06- 211072-5 (pbk.)

19 20 SCP 10 ❖ First Edition

I Can Read!

SHARED My First READING

Pete the Cat

Pete at the Beach

by James Dean

HARPER
An Imprint of HarperCollins Publishers

It is a hot day!
Pete the cat goes to the beach
with his mom and his brother, Bob.

"Let's go in the water,"
Bob says.

"Maybe later," says Pete.

Bob likes to surf.

He rides the big waves.

It looks like fun.

"I'm hot," says Pete.

"Go in the water," says Mom.

"Maybe later," says Pete.

Pete makes a sand castle.

His mom helps him dig.

Here comes a big wave.

And there goes Pete.

Oh, no!

Where did his sand castle go?

Bob rides a big wave.

"Wow!" says Pete.

"That looks like fun."

Pete and his mom take a walk.

They find seashells.

They see a crab.

Pete's feet get wet.

His feet feel cool.

The rest of him is hot.

It is time for lunch.

Pete eats a sandwich.

He drinks lemonade.

The sun is very hot.

And Pete is very, very hot.

Bob is wet and cool.

"Let's play ball," says Pete.

"No, thanks," says Bob.

"I want to surf."

Pete throws the ball.

His mom catches it.

"Let's get our feet wet,"
says Mom.
"Well, okay," says Pete.

The water is cool.

It feels good.

Pete goes in deeper.

Bob waves to Pete.
"I want to show you
how to surf!" he yells.

Pete does not say
"Maybe later."
He says, "Let's do it!"

"Lie on the board," says Bob.

Pete lies on the board.

"Paddle," says Bob.

Pete paddles out.

He waits for a big wave.

A big wave is coming!

"Stand up!" says Bob.

Pete stands up.

25

Then Pete falls down.

It was scary,

but it did not hurt.

"Try again later," says Bob.

Pete wants to try again now.

Pete lies down again.

He paddles out and waits.

Here comes a wave!

Pete stands up.

This time he rides the wave!

"Good job," says Bob.

Pete wants to surf all day.

Bob does, too.

So they take turns.

Pete and Bob rock and roll
with the waves.
What a great day!

It is okay to be afraid.

But it is more fun to surf!